For Ellie Berger

CHAPTERS

CAPTAIN UnderPANTS: The 100% TRUE TRUTH!!!

once upon a Time there was two COOL Kids named George and Harold.

They were ~~be a~~ smart and handsome and stuff.

Thank you, Yes, we know.

me Too!

But they had the meanest Principal ever. Name of Mr. Krupp.

BLah BLah BLah!

One time, Mr. Krupp was being mean.

You will FOLLOW my RULES!

So They hypnotized him.

Not Today, BuB!!!

Mr. Krupp was under George and Harold's Spell.

You are now Captain Underpants.

OK

It was funny at first...

HA HA HA HA HA HA HA HA

Look at me!

But it got really dangerous really quick!!!

Tra-la Laaaaa!

Then one day, Mr. Krupp drank some alien super power juice...

Alien super Power Juice

... and he got REAL super powers!

Now, whenever Mr. Krupp Hears somebody snap their fingers......

SNAP

...he turns into captain underpants.

Tra-La Laaaaa!

and whenever Captain Underpants gets water on his head....

...he turns back into Mr. Krupp.

Blah Blah Blah!

so we got **THAT** to deal with.

But it gets **worse!!!**

One Day George and Harold had a really BIG Problem.

I GOT YOU **NOW!!!**

So They ~~stole~~ Borrowed a Time machine...

...and they went Back in time to Fix the Problem.

HOORAY!

we're smart

But They created a Totally New Problem!

OH No!!!

We ~~a~~ made **DOUBLES** of ourselves!

when their teachers Saw **TWO** Georges and **TWO** Harolds, They all went **CRAZY!!!**

we must be Dreaming!!!

Let's get NEKKiD!!!

So they all had to go to the 🐛 hospital.

The only **GOOD** thing that happened is that we got three new pets...

They are ½ Bionic hamsters and ½ Pterodactyls.

IT's Been a Few weeks since our Last adventure...

...The city has Been Rebuilt...

...and things are getting back To Normal.

But there are still a Lots OF Loose ends to OUR STORY!

That can oNLY mean one Thing:

another SEQUeL!

OH NO!

Here we go again!

CHAPTER 1
GEORGE AND GEORGE
AND HAROLD AND HAROLD

This is George Beard and George Beard and
Harold Hutchins and Harold Hutchins. George
and George are the kids on the left with the
ties and the flat-tops. Harold and Harold are
the ones on the right with the T-shirts and
the bad haircuts. Remember that now.

CHAPTER 2
THE GOP GUARANTEE*

If you read our last adventure, you're probably
well aware of how George and Harold accidentally
created duplicate versions of themselves.
You know all the whys, the whens, and the
wherefores, so you're all caught up and ready
to go. Congratulations! Good for you. Reading
is power, ain't it?

If you *didn't* read our last adventure, you're
probably scratching your head and saying to
yourself, "Hey, myself, what the heck is going
on here?"

*Some restrictions may apply. Void where prohibited.

Before we get into all of that, I should point out that it's impolite to use the word *heck*. These books have been criticized for their inappropriate language, and we're going to put a stop to that sort of thing once and for all. From now on**, you won't be reading any more words like *heck*, or *tinkle*, or *fart*, or *pee-pee*. No, sir! Those words are highly offensive to grouchy old people who have way too much time on their hands.

**Except on pages 44 and 48.

In the interest of pleasing all the grouchy old people (GOP) out there, I have also included topics especially for them. So this adventure will contain references to health care, gardening, Bob Evans Restaurants, hard candies, FOX News, and gentle-yet-effective laxatives.

So sit back (on your hemorrhoid pillows), turn up some music (Lawrence Welk), and grab a snack (black jelly beans that are all stuck together). It's time to enjoy the all-new, squeaky-clean, fully appropriate, and NON-offensive adventures of Captain Underpants!

CHAPTER 3
THE SPECIES WHO KNEW TOO MUCH

We all know that it's good to be smart. It's even better to be *very* smart. But being TOO smart is just asking for trouble. Take human beings for example: We were smart enough to invent gardening and health care, we developed Bob Evans Restaurants and FOX News, and we've managed to take hard candies and gentle-yet-effective laxatives to exciting new horizons. But somewhere along the way, we got TOO smart for our own good. We started inventing dumb things like car alarms, leaf blowers, and spray-on hair.

You'd think that *dumb* things would have been good enough for us, but no. Our big, ridiculous brains just weren't satisfied. We had to take things one step further. So we began creating incredibly *dangerous* things like atomic bombs and nuclear warheads, and we built enough of them to wipe out everybody on the planet. Then, like the smarty-pantses we are, we handed the launch codes over to politicians.

Only human beings are smart enough to be that dumb!

It turns out that brains are a lot like beans. They're both good, but you really don't want to overdo it with either one. You see, too much of a good thing usually ends up being a *VERY BAD* thing. One way or another, you're probably going to end up with a big, stinky mess.

The story you are about to read is the unfortunate tale of how the smartest brain on the planet created the biggest, stinkiest mess the world has ever seen. But before I can tell you that story, I have to tell you *this* story . . .

CHAPTER 4
SMART EARTH

As any scientist will tell you, we exist in an ever-expanding multiverse with an infinite number of stars and planets.

One of those planets, which orbits around the center star in Orion's Belt, is called Smart Earth. Smart Earth is almost identical to *our* Earth, except that everybody who lives on Smart Earth is a genius.

The reason everybody on Smart Earth
is so smart is that the entire planet is made
of an element called Zygo-Gogozizzle 24.
Zygo-Gogozizzle 24 is a slightly radioactive
substance that can bind with organic matter,
morph into complex organisms, and be
mixed with mayonnaise and dill-pickle
relish to create both a tasty salad dressing
and a clean-burning fuel source with enough
power to light up an entire city. One of the
remarkable side effects of being in close
proximity to Zygo-Gogozizzle 24 is that it
makes people much, *much* smarter than
they normally would be.

Even though Smart Earth is inhabited by geniuses, it still has a lot of similarities to *our* Earth. They've got McDonald's (though it's called "Smart McDonald's"), they have smartphones (which are called "smart smartphones"), and they've got the Huffington Post (which is called "the Huffington Post").

One day, a smart scientist at Smart Harvard University decided to do an experiment.

It was the smartest, most intelligent experiment that anyone on Smart Earth had ever conducted. It was so incredibly smart, in fact, that it ended up being totally dumb.

That afternoon in her laboratory, Smart Earth's smartest scientist mixed Smart Diet Coke with Smart Pop Rocks. Then she added a third ingredient to this highly volatile concoction: Smart Mentos.

This is what happened:

CHAPTER 5
LEGGO MY
ZYGO-GOGOZIZZLE 24

The explosion that followed sent chunks of Zygo-Gogozizzle 24 whizzing off in different directions throughout the galaxy and beyond.

One piece of Zygo-Gogozizzle 24 landed in a pond on the nearby planet Badpun, causing all of the pond water to turn into smart pond water.

PLiP

Soon the fish in the pond became *so* intelligent, they started swimming in schools.

Another piece of Zygo-Gogozizzle 24 ended up landing in a grape vineyard on planet Pinot. The Zygo-Gogozizzle 24 was quickly absorbed into the soil and was subsequently soaked up into the grapes.

These grapes, which had until recently been harvested almost to extinction, suddenly became self-aware and super intelligent. They banded together in bunches and rose up to defeat their oppressors.

The battle lasted one whole night, but sadly, it ended the next morning when the sun came up. The rebellion shriveled when the poor grapes ran out of juice. Apparently, there's a raisin for everything.

Perhaps the most devastating result of
the destruction of Smart Earth, however,
occurred when a tiny piece of Zygo-Gogozizzle
24 entered our *own* planet's atmosphere.
It soared down through the sky at a terrific
speed, zooming closer and closer to the
small midwestern town of Piqua, Ohio.

Finally, the tiny chunk of Zygo-Gogozizzle 24 crashed through the roof of the Piqua Valley Home for the Reality-Challenged. It landed in the group-therapy ward, where all of the teachers from the nearby elementary school had recently been transferred.

"What's that?" cried Mr. Krupp.

"Looks like a meteorite," said Ms. Ribble.

"Don't touch it," warned the doctor. "It might be *the Blob*!"

The doctor's warning was heeded by everyone except for the gym teacher, Mr. Meaner. Gym teachers, as I'm sure you are all aware, are a lot like toddlers. You really have to keep an eye on them, because they're always picking things up off the floor and putting them in their mouths.

Unfortunately, that's exactly what happened
on that fateful day at the Piqua Valley Home
for the Reality-Challenged.

"Mmmmmm," said Mr. Meaner, as he
happily chewed up the Zygo-Gogozizzle 24
and swallowed hard. "Tastes like chicken!"

CHAPTER 6
THE TROUBLE
WITH ZIZZLES

Suddenly, the tiny chunk of Zygo-Gogozizzle 24 began to bind with Mr. Meaner's stomach lining. It started taking over his cells at an alarming rate, spreading throughout his squishy innards and overriding his normal bodily functions. Soon, the Zygo-Gogozizzle 24 reached Mr. Meaner's mind, where it supercharged all of his brain cells and began the complicated process of making him smart.

"Are you alright, Mr. Meaner?" asked the psychologist. "You look a little strange."

"I'm much more than *alright*," replied Mr. Meaner. "I'm exceptionally impeccable!"

Mr. Meaner's fellow teachers looked worried. They had never heard him use anything larger than a three-syllable word before. Usually, Mr. Meaner just pointed at things and grunted.

"Er, I think you'd better sit down," said the psychologist.

"Nonsense, my good man," said Mr. Meaner, as his mind's neurons and glial cells began restructuring themselves, forming new connections and making his brain smarter and smarter each second. "I've wasted far too much time in this insipid infirmary already."

"Now, wait just a minute," said the psychologist. "You can't leave here. You're a patient."

"On the contrary," said Mr. Meaner, who now spoke in a standard British accent. "I shall walk right out that door expeditiously, and neither you nor anyone else is going to stop me."

"HELP! EMERGENCY!" shouted the psychologist. "We've got a runner!"

Another doctor rushed in to help. Together, the two doctors blocked the exit and refused to budge.

"You're not going anywhere, bub!" said the psychologist.

Mr. Meaner smirked as he looked at the two doctors with pity. This was going to be *too easy*.

CHAPTER 7
A PARADOX
FOR A PAIR OF DOCS

Mr. Meaner approached the two doctors.

"I have some advice for both of you," said Mr. Meaner.

"Well, too bad," said the psychologist. "Because we're not going to follow *any* of your advice!"

"Is that so?" asked Mr. Meaner. "Then I advise you to *NOT* follow my advice!"

The two doctors were confused.

"W-well, we're *not* going to follow that advice," said the psychologist.

"But if we *don't* follow his advice to *not* follow his advice," said the other doctor, "then aren't we *following* his advice?"

"Wait a minute," said the psychologist. "What if we follow his advice to *NOT* follow his advice? Are we still following his advice?"

The two doctors became so entangled in their deep, paradoxical conversation that they didn't even notice Mr. Meaner walking out the exit door.

"Hey, now's our chance to escape, too," said Ms. Ribble. The other teachers followed her out the door, right past the increasingly confused and frustrated doctors.

All of the teachers and staff of Jerome Horwitz Elementary School were now free. They followed Mr. Meaner up to the hilltop and watched him in awe as he looked out over the horizon.

Most people in Mr. Meaner's position would use their newfound genius brains to end world hunger and bring peace to humanity. But these were the last things on Mr. Meaner's magnificent mind.

Mr. Meaner was still a gym teacher at heart, you see. And as everyone knows, most gym teachers are inherently evil.

CHAPTER 8
WHY CAN'T WE BE FIENDS?

"It occurs to me," said Mr. Meaner, "that our recent problems have all been caused by willful and disobedient children."

"I heard that!" said Mr. Krupp.

"SILENCE, YOU FOOL!" Mr. Meaner shouted. "If we are to rectify this aberration, we must proceed with prudence and acumen!"

"I'm not sure what those words mean," said Miss Anthrope, "but I agree one hundred and thirty-nine percent!"

"Me, too," said the other teachers simultaneously.

"Then you must follow my every command,"
said Mr. Meaner. "You must all return to your
jobs and go about your business as usual.
Nothing is to look suspicious."

"B-but we want to be evil, too," Mr. Rected
whined.

"Patience, my dear minions," said Mr.
Meaner with a hideous sneer. "There will be
plenty of time for that in the days to come!"

CHAPTER 9
CRIMES AND MR. MEANER

A few days later, school was back in session.
The teachers taught, the students studied . . .

STUDENT AND
TEACHER
ART FAIR
STARTS WED.

. . . and George and Harold went back to their mischief.

44

After school, George and Harold climbed
up into their tree house to do their homework.
The "yesterday" versions of themselves were
busy playing video games and reading comics.

"How was school today?" asked Yesterday
George.

"Meh," said George.

"Didja learn anything new?" asked
Yesterday Harold.

"Eh," said Harold, shrugging.

By all appearances, things had finally
returned to normal.

But at night, Mr. Meaner tinkered away at a makeshift laboratory inside an old, abandoned factory near Franz Pond. He was developing a powerful mind-control potion that would turn even the most unruly child into a brainlessly obedient conformist.

Using a base mixture of sodium thiopental, Mr. Meaner added liberal doses of butyric acid, tryptophan, and Clamato juice. Then he filtered the solution through an old, dirty pile of stinky gym socks. The concoction smelled terrible, but its sinister effect would be even worse!

"My formula is now ready for human trials," said Mr. Meaner. "And I know exactly *which two humans* I'm going to try it out on!"

CHAPTER 10
SPRAY DAY

The next day, Mr. Meaner showed up at school looking a little different than usual. He still wore the same smelly sweatshirt and sweatpants he'd had on all week—nothing new there—but somehow, something about him had changed.

It was Yesterday George and Yesterday Harold's turn to go to school and do homework that day, so the boys dutifully went to their classes and did everything they were supposed to do . . .

JOIN US FOR WEDNESDAY'S "MATH CHAT"

. . . and a few things they were *not* supposed to do.

Everything seemed normal until after gym class. Mr. Meaner excused the rest of the kids, but not Yesterday George and Yesterday Harold.

"Boys," said Mr. Meaner, "I'd like to see you in my office, pronto!"

"Why?" asked Yesterday George. "We didn't do anything—*probably*."

Mr. Meaner pointed to his office door. "IN—MY—OFFICE—NOW!" he shouted.

Yesterday George and Yesterday Harold slinked into Mr. Meaner's filthy office. They'd been in there before, and they hated the smell of it. It reeked of mold, rat urine, and the putrid sweat of a thousand tormented souls. But today, for some strange reason, it smelled even *worse* than usual.

Yesterday George and Yesterday Harold climbed into two sticky vinyl chairs and held their breath.

"Well, well, well," said Mr. Meaner, as he closed the door behind him and approached our heroes. "It looks like we're alone at last."

"What's going on here?" asked Yesterday George suspiciously.

"Yeah," said Yesterday Harold. "We've got to go to our next class."

"Oh, there will be plenty of time for classes and studying and homework," replied Mr. Meaner. "But first, I'd like you to help me out with a little experiment!"

Mr. Meaner lifted his arms, revealing two metallic spray nozzles under his crusty pits.

"Say hello to my stinky friends!" He laughed as the nozzles spattered out two brown cloudbursts of choking, noxious stank.

CHAPTER 11
ASLS
(ATTENTION SUPERFLUOUS LETHARGY SYNDROME)

You've probably all heard of ADHD. It's a condition known as Attention Deficit Hyperactivity Disorder. George and Harold had been diagnosed with it when they were in the second grade.

At the time, George's dad had explained to the boys that people with ADHD are usually more creative than ordinary people. This made George and Harold feel very special, and they wore their diagnoses like a badge of honor.

But today, as they walked down the hallway to their next class, the boys felt much different than normal. It was almost as if their ADHD had been dramatically *reversed* somehow. They felt focused and attentive. They were calm and orderly. They did not feel the uncontrollable urge to daydream or misbehave. Something had changed about them.

"YOU'RE LATE FOR CLASS!" shouted their math teacher, Anita Calculator.

"We are very sorry." said Yesterday Harold robotically.

"Just for that, I'm going to give you *EXTRA* homework!" Miss Calculator snarled.

"Thank you, dear teacher." said Yesterday George in an enthusiastic monotone. "That would be lovely!"

Miss Calculator eyed the two boys suspiciously as they found their way to their desks and sat down quietly. All through class, as she droned on and on, she observed the most peculiar thing she had ever seen. Yesterday George and Yesterday Harold were actually *sitting still and paying attention*. They weren't fidgeting, they weren't giggling, and they weren't drawing or talking or making irritating noises with their armpits. They had become *model students*.

"I don't know what you two boys are up to," said Miss Calculator at the end of class, "but I LIKE it!"

"Thank you," said Yesterday George. "Our greatest desire is to please you."

"That is right," said Yesterday Harold. "And thank you for all the extra homework, too. We will do our very best!"

Even Melvin Sneedly was impressed. "Those guys are cooler than I thought," said Melvin.

All through the day, Yesterday George and Yesterday Harold were making quite an impression on the faculty of Jerome Horwitz Elementary School. The teachers couldn't believe it when the two boys walked right past a bulletin board without changing the letters around.

"They could have easily rearranged those letters to read: *Our Cafeteria Makes You Barf*," said Ms. Guided. "But they didn't!"

"I don't know what's going on with those two kids," said Miss Labler, "but I LIKE it!"

At the end of the school day, Yesterday George and Yesterday Harold went around to each classroom, asking if they could do extra-credit homework that evening. The teachers gladly piled it on.

"I don't know what you did to those two brats today," said Mr. Krupp, "but I LIKE it!"

"This is only the beginning," Mr. Meaner sneered. "Today I changed George and Harold. Soon, I shall change the world!"

Unlike most megalomaniacs, Mr. Meaner had no interest in taking over the planet. He was smarter than that. He knew that the *real* money and power was in pharmaceuticals. Mr. Meaner had created a formula that transformed children into highly attentive, obedient servants. All he needed to do was mass market his creation, and he would become the most powerful entity on Earth.

"Adults will pay through the NOSE for that kind of thing," he said with a laugh, petting Mr. Krupp's head affectionately. "But for now, the first taste is free."

CHAPTER 12
MEN AT WORK

That afternoon, Yesterday George and Yesterday Harold climbed up into the tree house with so much homework, they had to make two trips to hoist it all up.

"WHOA!" shouted George. "What happened today?!!?"

"It was a great day." said Yesterday Harold. "The teachers were so kind, they gave us seventeen pounds of homework!"

"*SEVENTEEN POUNDS OF HOMEWORK?!!?*" shouted Harold. "WE'RE *DOOMED!*"

"No. we are not." said Yesterday George. "We can all work on it together. It will be *fun!*"

George and Harold looked at each other in horror. Never in a million years would they have used the words *homework* and *fun* in the same sentence. Something was wrong. Something was terribly, terribly wrong.

"Are you thinking what I'm thinking?" whispered George.

"Body snatchers," whispered Harold.

"Yep," whispered George.

The four boys sat at their table and began tackling their assignments. Yesterday George and Yesterday Harold plowed through page after page of worksheets and take-home quizzes at a dizzying rate. George and Harold tried to keep up, but they kept getting distracted.

At suppertime, Yesterday George and Yesterday Harold went down to their homes to eat with their families. An hour later, they went back up to the tree house to continue their work.

"We brought some extra food for you." said Yesterday Harold.

"Thanks," said George and Harold.

Everyone worked until it was time for bed.

"We have completed our half to the best of our ability." said Yesterday George.

George and Harold hadn't even made a dent in their half.

"We're gonna be working on this all night!" moaned Harold.

"I have a satisfactory suggestion." said Yesterday George. "You two boys finish your work tonight, and we will go to school *again* tomorrow."

"Really?" said George. "You'll go to school *TWO DAYS IN A ROW*?!!?"

"Nobody should have to endure *that*," cried Harold.

"We do not mind." said Yesterday George and Yesterday Harold simultaneously. "We *LOVE* school!"

So while Yesterday George and Yesterday Harold slept in their beds, George and Harold stayed up until 5:00 A.M. answering questions, filling in blanks, and showing their work.

"Man, I'm wiped out!" said George. "If this keeps up, we're going to get sick."

"I'm already getting sick," said Harold, as he blew his nose.

CHAPTER 13
THE STINKY-KONG 2000

The next day, Mr. Meaner looked even *more* different than he had the day before. He'd been building a mechanical suit in his laboratory, and each new morning it got more and more elaborate. The genius gym teacher started the day by spraying all of the children in his classes with his newest mind-control formula, Rid-O-Kid 2000™.

"Say hello to my stinky friends!" shouted Mr. Meaner with each squirt.

In no time at all, the entire student body of Jerome Horwitz Elementary School was transformed. Now *every* kid in school had Attention Superfluous Lethargy Syndrome.

"This is WONDERFUL!" Mr. Krupp exclaimed. "There's no more laughing, no more daydreaming, and no more running or playing or goofing around. It's like you've crushed their spirits *AND* their imaginations in one fell swoop!"

"I'm really doing the world a great service," Mr. Meaner said with a slithery smile. "I'm raising a new generation of totally compliant button-pushers. They'll do what they're told, they won't question authority, and best of all, NO COMPLAINING!"

"Yeah, but isn't Rid-O-Kid 2000™ dangerous?" asked Ms. Ribble.

"Not for us," said Mr. Meaner. "The spray only affects children. Adults are totally immune, so it's perfectly safe!"

The only downside to Mr. Meaner's intranasally absorbed spray is that it only lasted for twenty-four hours. To be completely effective, it needed to be resprayed every day.

"That's the beauty of my system," said Mr. Meaner. "Once parents see how easy it is to control children, they'll pay ANYTHING for a daily *fix*!"

CHAPTER 14
AND NOW, A WORD
FROM OUR SPONSOR . . .

As the week progressed, George and Harold
got more and more swamped with homework.
They stayed up later and later each night and
got sicker and sicker.

"Let's take a break and watch some TV," said
George one morning, as he wiped his nose.

"OK," said Harold, with a sneeze.

George turned on the TV and flipped
through the channels. Suddenly, he saw a
familiar face.

"HEY!" shouted Harold. "That's Mr.
Meaner!"

"What's *HE* doing on TV?" cried George.
He turned up the volume, and the two boys
watched Mr. Meaner's commercial in horror.

Are your kids annoying?

Do they fight and whine and complain all the time?

Do they refuse to eat anything but macaroni and cheese?

Are they sucking the LIFE out of you?

Well, Rid-O-Kid 2000™ is here to help.

Our scientifically proven formula will transform even the most willful child into an obedient, respectful, and hardworking servant—er, I mean, angel.

And Rid-O-Kid 2000™ has a full day's supply of Vitamin C, so you can feel GOOD about dosing your child with a narcotic that has never been tested for long-term effects.

So turn your brat into a brown-noser . . . with Rid-O-Kid 2000™.

"I KNEW something was wrong," said Harold, "but it looks even worse than I'd imagined!"

"We'd better go to school and get to the bottom of this!" said George.

"But we're sick," cried Harold. "I can't even breathe through my nose!"

"Me neither," said George. "But a kid's gotta do what a kid's gotta do!"

CHAPTER 15
DISGUISE FALLING

George and Harold rummaged through their houses until they found what they needed. There was no way they were going to show up at school looking like *themselves* again. They'd learned that lesson in our last book. George and Harold needed a disguise, and it needed to be convincing.

When they arrived at school, George changed into his costume behind the bushes and climbed onto Harold's shoulders. Then they headed into the building. Normally, any stranger entering Jerome Horwitz Elementary School would need to sign in at the office and go through a security screening. But George and Harold noticed that things at school were a little more *relaxed* today.

Their first clue was that there were no adults in the office. At least it looked that way. Upon closer inspection, they discovered that the school secretary, Miss Anthrope, was sound asleep on the floor under her desk. Some third graders were giving her a foot massage, while the sixth-grade AV club was answering the phone and filing papers.

"That's weird," said George.

As George and Harold walked down the hallway, things just got weirder and weirder. First, they noticed a brownish haze in the air.

"I wonder what that brown fog is all about," said George.

"I don't know," said Harold. "I can't smell a thing because of my cold."

"Me neither," said George.

As they roamed from room to room, they noticed that the other teachers were asleep, too, and their students were doing all sorts of odd things for them. Some kids were giving the teachers massages, and others were shaving their teachers' beards, plucking their eyebrows, and giving them haircuts.

The mathletes were filling out the teachers' tax forms, while the shop kids were washing all the cars in the faculty parking lot.

Finally, George and Harold reached the cafeteria, where several teachers were lying on the lunch tables getting Ashiatsu massages and mani-pedis at the same time.

"Boy, things sure have gotten a lot better around this place since Rid-O-Kid 2000™ came along!" said Ms. Zurry.

"I'll say," said Ms. Guided. "I was happy enough when my students were finally able to sit still and pay attention all day. But when I found out that they'd follow my every command without question, it changed my life!"

"Mine, too," said Mr. Rected. "I just sent my whole class over to my home. They're mowing my lawn, watering my garden, and painting my house as we speak!"

The three teachers all had a good laugh and drifted off into a relaxing, dreamy sleep.

"Oh, NO!" cried George. "The teachers have turned all the kids into mindless servants!"

"We'd better get out of here before they turn *us* into servants, too," said Harold.

"OK," said George, with a wicked smile.
"But first, let's have a little fun."

CHAPTER 16
HAPPY PRANKSGIVING

"If all the kids in school are blindly following the orders of adults," said George, "then maybe they'll follow OUR orders, too, since we're *dressed* like an adult."

"That makes sense," said Harold. "Let's order everyone to *STOP* following orders!"

"Nah," said George. "We've already used that joke in this book. I've got a better idea!"

So George and Harold went around the school whispering *NEW* orders to all of the students. First, they whispered some new orders to the kids who were giving out free shaves and haircuts.

"Are you sure?" asked the children.

"Of course I'm sure," said George. "I'm an authority figure!"

"Very well, sir," said the children.

Next, they whispered some new orders to the kids who were filling out tax forms.

"Are you sure?" asked the children.

"I'm an adult!" said George. "Don't question me!"

"Alright, sir," said the children.

Then they passed out permanent markers
to another group of kids, and whispered some
new orders to them, too.

"Are you SURE?" asked the children.

"Absolutely!" said George. "I'm a grown-up.
I don't make mistakes!"

"As you wish." said the children.

The rest of the afternoon continued in
much the same way, with George and Harold
dishing out new orders to every kid they came
across.

"We'd better get out of here," said Harold.
"Those teachers are going to wake up pretty
soon, and they're not going to be very happy!"

"OK," said George. "We can do the last one
on our way home."

As they headed back to their tree house,
George and Harold stopped by Mr. Rected's
place. His whole yard was filled with children
mowing the lawn, watering the flower garden,
and painting the house. George whispered
some new orders to them as well.

"Are you SURE?!!?" asked the children.

"Sure, we're sure," said George. "I mean,
'Sure, *I'M* sure.' Don't use your brains. Just
follow orders!"

CHAPTER 17
WAKEY WAKEY,
BIG MISTAKEY

George and Harold walked back to their tree house feeling pretty good about themselves. But things were not looking so good for the teachers at school, who were just waking up.

"Hey!" shouted Miss Anthrope. "Somebody drew on my face with permanent markers while I was asleep!"

"Mine, too!" shouted Miss Fitt. "And they spray-painted my *rear end*!"

"Someone gave me a Mohawk!" cried Ms. Ribble.

"Somebody shaved off my eyebrows and *Goofy-Glued* them to my chin!" wailed Ms. Zurry.

"Somebody filled out my tax forms in *pig Latin* and mailed them to the IRS!" screamed Miss Labler.

Ms. Dayken rushed to the mirror. "Thank goodness nobody did anything to me." She laughed. "Hooray!"

"Don't look now," cried Mr. Rustworthy, "but a bunch of kids are out in the parking lot filling up our cars with low-fat cottage cheese!"

The teachers all rushed to the windows.

"WHAT IS THE MEANING OF THIS?!!!?" they shouted.

"We are following orders." said one of the children.

"WHO GAVE YOU THOSE ORDERS?" screamed Mr. Krupp.

"An authority figure." said another kid. "We *never* question authority figures."

The teachers were outraged. They
marched across town to the old, abandoned
building that Mr. Meaner had converted into
a Rid-O-Kid 2000™ spray-can factory.

"LOOK WHAT THOSE KIDS DID TO US!"
Mr. Krupp shouted at Mr. Meaner. "That
stupid, stinky spray of yours doesn't work!"

"That's impossible," said Mr. Meaner. "I'm
going to get to the bottom of this."

CHAPTER 18
LOW-FAT RIDER

Mr. Meaner ran back to school, climbed into his low-fat-cottage-cheese-filled car, and drove around the city. Even with his massive, intelligent brain, he still couldn't figure out what had gone wrong.

As he drove, he passed by a curious sight.
A group of children were watering someone's
house, mowing their flower garden, and
painting their lawn. Mr. Meaner stopped his
car and got out.

"What on *EARTH* are you children doing?"
he asked.

"We are following orders." said one of
the kids.

"Who *ordered* you to do these things?"
asked Mr. Meaner.

"A grown-up." said the kid. "Grown-ups
do not make mistakes."

Mr. Meaner squished back into his car and peeled off.

"No adult would give those kinds of orders," Mr. Meaner concluded. "This HAS to be the work of a *CHILD*. And there's only one way to solve *that* problem!"

Mr. Meaner zoomed back to his factory and strapped himself into the Stinky-Kong 2000 Mecha-Suit he had been building all week.

"Somewhere in this town there are *children* hiding," Mr. Meaner said, "and I'm gonna *GIT* 'em!"

CHAPTER 19
LET US SPRAY

The genius gym teacher stomped out of his factory and headed down the street, spraying everything in sight with his hideous Mecha-Spray Armpits.

"SAY HELLO TO MY STINKY FRIENDS!" he shouted.

The horrible brown clouds rose up over the city, getting bigger and billowier as they spread out across the town. After several hours, George and Harold could see the brown clouds from their tree house window.

"There's that brown fog again," said George. "It won't be long before it reaches *our* neighborhood!"

"It's a good thing our noses are clogged up," said Harold. "We can't smell it, so we're immune."

"Yeah, but our colds won't last forever," said George. "I'm already starting to feel better."

"Uh-oh," said Harold. "We need to find an adult we can trust, and FAST!"

George and Harold had no other choice
but to ask their parents for help. The two
desperate boys sneaked into Harold's house,
where both of their families were sitting
together, just finishing up dinner.

"Thanks for inviting us over for supper,"
said George's dad.

"It's always a pleasure," said Harold's mom.

"Please let us clear the table." said
Yesterday George.

"What a splendid idea." said Yesterday
Harold. "Then we shall wash the dishes and
mop the floor! Oh, what fun we shall have!"

George and Harold hid in the hallway, waiting for just the right moment to come in and tell everyone their terrible tale of woe. But before they got a chance, their parents began to talk.

"I don't know what's come over those two boys lately," said George's dad, "but I LIKE it!"

"Me, too," said Harold's mom. "They've really grown up these past few days."

"It's like their whole personalities have changed," said George's mom. "What an *improvement*!"

George and Harold looked at each other with sadness . . .

. . . then walked back to their tree house, brokenhearted.

"Aw, man," said Harold. "Our parents like the *new* versions of us better than they like the *us* versions of us."

"We're going to have to find some adults we can REALLY trust," said George.

"But who?" cried Harold.

"I've got an idea," said George.

George and Harold ran across town through
the choking brown fog until they reached
Melvin Sneedly's house. Luckily, Melvin's garage
door was open. Even *luckilier*, Melvin's glow-
in-the-dark, time-traveling Robo-Squid suits
were there, too.

George climbed up into one of the cockpits
and fired up the engine. The Robo-Squid suit
lunged forward and grabbed Harold in its
tentacled arm. Then it slithered down the
sidewalk while George set the controllers.

"You know, we really shouldn't be taking this," said Harold. "It isn't ours."

"Technically, it *IS* ours," said George. "Melvin only had *one* of these things, and WE made the second one. You can't *steal* something you made yourself, can you?"

"That's a good point," said Harold.

George finished setting the controllers and pressed the "Start" button. The Robo-Squid suit shook and sputtered, then disappeared into a ball of blinding light.

CHAPTER 20
AWAY WE GO!

George and Harold were instantly transported twenty years into the future. Quickly, they ran up to an old lady sitting with her twenty-three-year-old son.

"Look, son," said the old lady. "A giant glow-in-the-dark robotic squid is carrying a little boy in one of its tentacles!"

"*Sure* it is, Mom," said her son. "Listen, you need to take your medication EVERY DAY or it's not going to—"

"Excuse me," said George.

The twenty-three-year-old looked up from his phone and screamed, "AAAAAH! IT'S A GIANT GLOW-IN-THE-DARK ROBOTIC SQUID CARRYING A LITTLE BOY IN ONE OF ITS TENTACLES!"

"Uh, yeah," said George. "Look, we need to borrow your phone. We're trying to locate George Beard."

"You mean the author?" said the guy.

"D-Did you say *AUTHOR*?!!?" cried George excitedly.

"Yeah," said the guy. "Everybody knows George Beard. He writes those Dog Man graphic novels."

"NO WAY!!!" screamed George. He was so overcome with happiness, he couldn't contain himself. The glow-in-the-dark, time-traveling Robo-Squid suit jumped up and down, spun around, and danced a happy jig. "I WRITE GRAPHIC NOVELS IN THE FUTURE!!!" screamed George. "OH YEAH!!! I WRITE GRAPHIC NOVELS IN THE FUTURE!!!"

"Settle down," cried Harold, who was starting to feel ill from all the dancing and jerking around. "You're acting too crazy, man. Show a little self-control, OK?!!?"

"Sorry," said George, setting Harold down.

"Do you know where Mr. Beard lives?" George asked the guy.

"Yeah, he lives up there on Echo Hills next to that graphic novel artist," said the guy. "I think his name is . . . um . . . Harold *Hutchings* or something."

"*I'M* HAROLD HUTCHINGS OR SOMETHING!" screamed Harold, as he jumped up and down, flipped somersaults, and ran around in circles like a crazy person. "I ILLUSTRATE GRAPHIC NOVELS IN THE FUTURE! OH BABY!!! I ILLUSTRATE GRAPHIC NOVELS IN THE FUTURE!"

"C'mon, *Mr. Self-Control*," said George. "Let's go meet our future selves!"

CHAPTER 21
IT'S NICE TO MEET ME

George and Harold could hardly contain themselves as they rang the doorbell of George's future self. They were so excited, they'd almost forgotten why they had come to the future in the first place.

Soon, George's future self came to the door. He looked a lot like George, only he was really, really old. He was *THIRTY*!

Old George recognized George and Harold immediately.

"HOLY *TOLEDO*!" cried Old George. "Wh-What are *you guys* doing here?"

Old George's wife came to the door, too. "Don't be rude to your fans, honey," she said. "Invite them in! Make yourselves at home, boys."

"These aren't my fans, dear," said Old George. "They're US!"

"Us *who*?" asked Mrs. Beard.

"It's Harold and me from when we were kids," said Old George.

George and Harold accepted Mrs. Beard's invitation and made themselves right at home. They gleefully tore through the house, checking out all of Old George's stuff.

"Your future house is *AWESOME*!" said Harold.

"Thanks," said George. "I must admit, I have pretty good taste!"

"WOW!" cried Harold. "You've even got your own PINBALL MACHINE!!!"

"COOL!" exclaimed George. "I've always wanted one!"

"Can I play it?" asked Harold.

"I guess so," said George. "After all, it's *mine*."

"Look, Harold," cried George. "There's
even a tree house in my backyard!"

"Er, that's not for *us*," said Old George.
"That's for our kids."

"Our *KIDS*?!!?" asked George.

"I guess it's time you boys met the whole
family," said Mrs. Beard. "I'll go round up
the children, honey, while you call Harold
and Billy."

CHAPTER 22
THE GANG'S ALL HERE

Soon, everyone had gathered together in Old George's studio. Old George, his wife, and their kids, Meena and Nik, sat on the couch, while Old Harold, his husband, and their twins, Owen and Kei, plopped down in the giant beanbag chair.

"Kids," said Mrs. Beard, "I'd like you to meet your fathers."

"What's up?" said George.

"We're your dads when they were kids," said Harold.

"Wow, Dad," said Meena. "You used to be cute!"

"Whaddaya mean, *used to be*?!!?" said Old George.

"We're here because we need to borrow your dads," said Harold. "They're the only adults we can trust!"

"Yeah," said George. "It's a real emergency!"

"Wait a minute," said Old Harold. "I don't remember doing any of this when we were kids, do you, George?"

"No," said Old George. "If *this* happened in our past, how come *we* have no memory of it?"

"I don't know," said Harold.

"Probably bad writing," said George.

"Well, if we're going to help you, we'd better get going," said Old George. "Let's boogie!"

"But wait," said Harold. "We need to finish our pinball game."

"Yeah," said George. "And we haven't even read your graphic novels yet."

"I thought this was an *emergency*," said Old Harold.

"How about just ONE chapter?" Harold begged. *"Pleeeeeease?"*

"Well, alright," said Old Harold.

George and Harold grabbed a graphic
novel from the bookshelf, flipped it open, and
started reading from a random chapter.

115

CHAPTER 23
DOG MAN:
THE RANDOM CHAPTER

BECAUSE I'M NOT DOG MAN!

FLiNG

RUSTLE RUSTLE

ACTUALLY, I'M PETEY, THE WORLD'S MOST INCORRIGIBLE CAT!

PETEY?!!? I THOUGHT YOU WERE DEAD!

THAT'S WHAT I *WANTED* YOU TO THINK!

BUT WHAT HAPPENED TO DOG MAN?

DOG MAN IS THE ONE WHO IS DEAD . . .

MY VENUS-FLYTRAP MONKEYS HAVE SURELY FINISHED HIM OFF BY NOW!

SHONG

AND NOW, DEAR COPPERS, IT IS *YOUR* TURN TO DIE!

HEY, YOU BROKE MY SWORD!

YOU OWE ME SIXTEEN BUCKS!

THAT'S WHAT I *WANTED* YOU TO THINK!

AND NOW YOU SHALL WITNESS THE DEFEAT OF THE BARK KNIGHT!

NOT IF I CAN HELP IT!

MILLY, DON'T BE A HERO!

DON'T BE A FOOL WITH YOUR LIFE!

MY MASK!

HEY! YOU'RE NOT MECHA-PETEY!

NO! THIS WHOLE TIME IT'S BEEN ME: FLIPPY! THE WORLD'S MOST SINISTER PSYCHOKINETIC FISH!

FLIPPY?!!? I THOUGHT HE WAS DEAD!

THAT'S WHAT I *WANTED* YOU TO THINK!

TO BE CONTINUED . . .

CHAPTER 24
AWAY WE GO (AGAIN)!

"Well?" said Old George. "What did you think? Did you like it?"

"I guess so," said Harold.

"Yeah," said George. "It was pretty good — for old people."

"PRETTY GOOD?!!?" cried Old Harold.

"*OLD* PEOPLE?!!?" cried Old George.

"Alright, let's boogie!" said George, as he went to the front yard and powered up the Robo-Squid suit. Quickly, he reached out three mechanical arms and picked up Harold, Old Harold, and Old George.

Suddenly, everything began to shake and sputter as a massive ball of electric light enveloped them all.

"Are you guys ready to go?" asked Harold.

"PRETTY GOOD?!!?" whined Old Harold.

"*OLD* PEOPLE?!!?" whined Old George.

As our heroes began to disappear into the shifting paradigms of time, they waved good-bye to their frightened families.

"Don't worry, kids," shouted George. "We'll all be back by chapter 38!"

CHAPTER 25
IT WAS TWENTY YEARS
AGO TODAY . . .

Everything stopped suddenly, and George,
Harold, and their future selves looked down
from the vacant hilltop. They were back in the
present, and the entire city below them was
surrounded by a gigantic, stinky brown cloud.

Quickly, they made their way through the
dark clouds to their tree house.

"WOW!" cried Old George. "I haven't been up here in years."

"Look," cried Old Harold. "It's Tony, Orlando, and Dawn. I remember them!"

"Yeah, whatever happened to them?" said Old George. "It was like they just *disappeared* one day!"

"I don't know what you're talking about," said Harold. "They've always been here, ever since they hatched."

"Listen, boys," said Old George. "You need to stay up here. We'll take care of Mr. Meaner and his stinky gas."

"Yeah," said Old Harold. "It's up to the *adults* to save the world this time!"

134

CHAPTER 26
STINKALICIOUS

The first thing that Old George and Old Harold did was run to Mr. Krupp's house.

Unfortunately, Mr. Meaner was walking down Mr. Krupp's street at that very moment in his Stinky-Kong 2000 Mecha-Suit, blowing brown, putrid fog throughout the neighborhood. Old George rang Mr. Krupp's doorbell, panicking. Suddenly, Mr. Krupp swung the front door open. He'd been at his kitchen sink all evening, scrubbing the permanent marker off of his face.

"What do *YOU* people want?!!?" shouted Mr. Krupp.

"We need the help of an old friend," said Old Harold, snapping his fingers.

SNAP!

"WELL?!!?" Mr. Krupp screamed. *"ANSWER ME!!!"*

Old George and Old Harold looked at each other in shock.

"It didn't work!" cried Old Harold. They both snapped their fingers this time.

SNAP! SNAP! SNAP! SNAP! SNAP! SNAP!

"HEY!" Mr. Krupp screamed. "Quit snapping your fingers in my face, you weirdos!"

Mr. Meaner and his Stinky-Kong 2000 Mecha-Suit were getting closer.

The whole street shook with every forceful stomp of his metallic monkey feet. Old George and Old Harold continued snapping their fingers feverishly.

"Why isn't it working?" cried Old Harold as he snapped.

"It must be all that water that's on his face!" cried Old George. "That's gotta be what's keeping him from transforming!"

"LISTEN UP, YOU TWO *PSYCHOS*!" Mr. Krupp screamed. "You better get outta my yard before I call the COPS! You're supposed to be ADULTS, but you're acting like a couple of KIDS!"

Suddenly, Mr. Meaner stopped. *"Adults acting like kids?"* he said, turning his head slyly. He looked at Old George and Old Harold. His genius brain began to calculate rapidly as he eyed them up and down. Then his face widened with a sinister, foul-smelling smile.

"Adults who act like children would be immune to my Rid-O-Kid 2000™ spray," Mr. Meaner said. "So *THEY* must be the pranksters I've been looking for!"

Mr. Meaner stomped up to Old George and Old Harold and grabbed the two friends in the clenching claws of the Stinky-Kong 2000.

CHAPTER 27

THE INCREDIBLY GRAPHIC VIOLENCE CHAPTER, PART 1 (IN FLIP-O-RAMA™)

PILKEY® BRAND
O-RAMA

HERE'S HOW IT WORKS!

STEP 1

First, place your *left* hand inside the dotted lines marked "LEFT HAND HERE." Hold the book open *flat*.

STEP 2

Grasp the *right-hand* page with your right thumb and index finger (inside the dotted lines marked "RIGHT THUMB HERE").

STEP 3

Now *quickly* flip the right-hand page back and forth until the picture appears to be *animated*.

(For extra fun, try adding your own sound-effects!)

FLIP-O-RAMA 1

(pages 143 and 145)

Remember, flip *only* page 143.
While you are flipping, be sure you
can see the picture on page 143
and the one on page 145.
If you flip quickly, the two
pictures will start to look like
<u>one</u> *animated* picture.

Don't forget to
add your own sound-effects!

LEFT HAND HERE

THE FIRST TIME
EVER I PUNCHED
YOUR FACE

RIGHT
INDEX
FINGER
HERE

144

THE FIRST TIME EVER I PUNCHED YOUR FACE

FLIP-O-RAMA 2

(pages 147 and 149)

Remember, flip *only* page 147.
While you are flipping, be sure you
can see the picture on page 147
and the one on page 149.
If you flip quickly, the two
pictures will start to look like
<u>one</u> *animated* picture.

Don't forget to
add your own sound-effects!

LEFT HAND HERE

KILLING ME SOFTLY
WITH HIS KONG

RIGHT
INDEX
FINGER
HERE

KILLING ME SOFTLY
WITH HIS KONG

CHAPTER 28
DON'T GO BREAKING
MY SPINE

With the help of his Stinky-Kong 2000 Mecha-Suit, Mr. Meaner was victorious. He picked up Old George and Old Harold in his mighty metallic fist and began to squeeze.

"Hey, don't kill those guys," cried Mr. Krupp, as he dried his face on an old red towel with black dots on it. "You'll ruin my lawn!"

"He—he just dried his face!" Old Harold gasped. "Now's our chance!"

Old George and Old Harold reached out
weakly and snapped their fingers.

SNAP! SNAP!

Suddenly, a silly smile spread across Mr.
Krupp's freshly dried face.

Quickly, he tore off his clothes and tied his red towel around his neck. The battle of the century was about to begin.

CHAPTER 29

THE INCREDIBLY GRAPHIC
VIOLENCE CHAPTER
PART 2 (IN FLIP-O-RAMA)

FLIP-O-RAMA 3

(pages 155 and 157)

Remember, flip *only* page 155.
While you are flipping, be sure you
can see the picture on page 155
and the one on page 157.
If you flip quickly, the two
pictures will start to look like
<u>one</u> *animated* picture.

Don't forget to
add your own sound-effects!

LEFT HAND HERE

SOMEBODY DONE SOMEBODY'S KONG WRONG

RIGHT
THUMB
HERE

RIGHT
INDEX
FINGER
HERE

156

SOMEBODY DONE SOMEBODY'S KONG WRONG

FLIP-O-RAMA 4

(pages 159 and 161)

Remember, flip *only* page 159.
While you are flipping, be sure you
can see the picture on page 159
and the one on page 161.
If you flip quickly, the two
pictures will start to look like
<u>one</u> *animated* picture.

Don't forget to
add your own sound-effects!

LEFT HAND HERE

I FIGHT THE
KONGS THAT
MAKE THE WHOLE
WORLD STINK

I FIGHT THE
KONGS THAT
MAKE THE WHOLE
WORLD STINK

CHAPTER 30
PIQUA PRISON BLUES

The Stinky-Kong 2000 Mecha-Suit was destroyed, and soon Mr. Meaner found himself sitting in a cell at Piqua State Penitentiary. Warden Gordon Bordon Schmorden stopped by to have a word with Mr. Meaner.

"Well, well, well," said Warden Schmorden smugly. "It looks like your days of giving orders to people are OVER!"

"Go make me an egg-salad sandwich," said Mr. Meaner.

"OK," said Warden Schmorden. "Coming right up!"

"And don't forget the dill-pickle relish!" said Mr. Meaner.

"I wouldn't dream of forgetting that, sir," said Warden Schmorden.

Five minutes later, Warden Gordon Bordon
Schmorden returned with a lovely egg-salad
sandwich loaded with dill-pickle relish.
Mr. Meaner grabbed it and scarfed it all down.

Suddenly, Mr. Meaner's body began to
change. The mayonnaise and the dill-pickle
relish began to combine with the Zygo-
Gogozizzle 24 that had taken over Mr.
Meaner's body. First, he began to vibrate and
glow, as tiny sparks of electricity shot out of
his fingers and toes. Then he started growing.

Mr. Meaner grew and grew and grew to such a gigantic size, he crashed out of his cell and pushed his way through the side of the jail.

Mr. Meaner had transformed into a highly intelligent blob of pure energy.

"I AM SIR STINKS-A-LOT!" he bellowed, as he zapped everything around him with cataclysmic crackles of electricity.

CHAPTER 31
OOZE ON DOWN THE ROAD

Sir Stinks-A-Lot slithered sloppily down the street looking for sweet, sweet revenge.

"Captain Underpants," he called mockingly, "come out and *PLAY-YAY*!"

Suddenly, Captain Underpants swooped in and smashed Sir Stinks-A-Lot right on the noggin with a telephone pole.

The gigantic evil blob zapped his lightning rays and swung his mighty fists, but Captain Underpants was just too quick.

Old George and Old Harold stood on the sidelines, cheering for the Waistband Warrior.

"Get him, Captain Underpants!" shouted Old George.

"Let's win this thing so we can all go home!" shouted Old Harold.

SPLAT!

Sir Stinks-A-Lot was getting very frustrated and annoyed. Then he thought of something really smart.

"Those two guys *seem* to know Captain Underpants pretty well," said Sir Stinks-A-Lot to himself. "I think it's time to find out EXACTLY what they know!"

Sir Stinks-A-Lot raised his terrifying fist above Old George and Old Harold . . .

. . . then clobbered them with a
powerful punch.

Quickly, the energy inside Sir Stinks-
A-Lot's body began to absorb Old George
and Old Harold. The two old friends began
to merge with the evil glob of energy,
and soon the three had become one.

"HAW! HAW! HAW!" laughed Sir Stinks-
A-Lot. "I've absorbed their bodies AND
their memories. Soon I'll know everything
that THEY know!"

Sir Stinks-A-Lot used his massive, glowing brain to quickly sort through Old George's and Old Harold's memories. He learned how they first met, he learned how they became friends, and he learned how they created Captain Underpants. Unfortunately, Sir Stinks-A-Lot also learned how to *DESTROY* Captain Underpants.

A sinister sneer stretched across the blobby face of the supremely intelligent super-villain. Swiftly, he oozed over to Franz Pond, chuckling maniacally to himself.

"You'd better let those guys go," shouted Captain Underpants, "or I'm gonna—"

"You're not going to do ANYTHING!"
screamed Sir Stinks-A-Lot, as he swooshed
his mighty hand into the pond and sent a
gigantic splash of water flying into the air.

CHAPTER 32
THE NIGHT THE LIGHTS
WENT OUT IN PIQUA

The massive spray of water hit Captain
Underpants with a powerful *ker-splooosh*.
Suddenly, our hero's confidence disappeared,
and he fell screaming from the sky.

"AAAAAAAAhhh!" he shrieked, as he tumbled to the ground and smashed into the earth with a terrifying sound effect

"Hey! I'm OK!" said Mr. Krupp, as he sat
up and dusted himself off.

"Wait a minute," shouted Sir Stinks-A-Lot.
"He's not even *hurt*! How could that be?!!?"

Sir Stinks-A-Lot reached down and
touched Mr. Krupp with one of his gigantic,
glowing fingers. A powerful burst of Zygo-
Gogozizzlistic energy zapped forth from his
massive fingertip and scanned Mr. Krupp's
body. Quickly, the villain's bulbous brain
analyzed each and every strand of DNA in Mr.
Krupp's body until a foreign substance was
detected.

"SO!" shouted Sir Stinks-A-Lot. "You've
got alien *Super Power Juice* in your DNA! I
guess I'll just have to extract it!"

Sir Stinks-A-Lot's finger grew brighter
and brighter as he performed one of the
most complicated laser surgeries ever: a
Super-Power-Juice-*ectomy*. Carefully, he
removed all of the super-powered elements
from Mr. Krupp's DNA and absorbed them
all into his massive, glowing body.

Mr. Krupp was unharmed, but he ran
home screaming anyway.

"Now I'VE got super powers!" laughed
Sir Stinks-A-Lot. "And now, I am truly
unstoppable!"

CHAPTER 33
I'M SENDIN' OUT
GOOD VIBRATIONS

What Sir Stinks-A-Lot failed to realize, however, was that Old George and Old Harold were still a part of him. Since they had all merged together, the two best friends' brains were now filled with super-powered Zygo-Gogozizzle 24.

It wasn't long before Old George and Old Harold had sorted through every particle of Zygo-Gogozizzle 24 and every glowing joule of energy that made up their hulkingly monstrous body.

Soon they knew everything, from the chemical makeup of their arch-enemy to the events that led to the destruction of Smart Earth. Old George and Old Harold oozed up from the back of Sir Stinks-A-Lot's head and started sending a message.

The two old friends thought as hard as they could, and soon, a telepathic signal radiated from their gooey heads to their old tree house, miles away.

Unfortunately, George and Harold were sound asleep. They didn't pick up the telepathic message at all.

Luckily, someone else did!

Tony, Orlando, and Dawn swooshed out
of the tree house and headed for a nearby
shopping center. The fate of the entire planet
was in their tiny paws.

CHAPTER 34
LAUGHTER MOON
DELIGHT

Sir Stinks-A-Lot had been victorious, and now it was time to gloat. "I've just defeated the world's greatest superhero! And now I'm the most intelligent, most powerful entity the world has ever SEEN!"

He oozed over to his Rid-O-Kid 2000™ factory and kissed it gently on the roof. "Soon, my stinky spray will take over the brains of all the children on Earth," he shouted. "I'll be their leader, and they'll gladly obey my every command!"

Sir Stinks-A-Lot threw back his hideously huge head and laughed and laughed and laughed. "HAW! HAW! HAW! HAW! HAW!"

CHAPTER 36
STUCK IN THE PUDDLE
WITH YOU

The terrible explosion blasted Sir Stinks-A-Lot's body apart, releasing a powerful electromagnetic pulse and launching the Super Power Juice and the Zygo-Gogozizzle 24 deep into outer space.

The factory was destroyed. The Rid-O-Kid 2000™ had disintegrated, and all that was left was a big, stinky mess.

A crowd of people gathered around Franz Pond to view the horrible glob of devastation.

Suddenly, the glob began to bubble and move. Then, Old George and Old Harold climbed out of its gooey center. They were completely unharmed.

"Hooray!" shouted the crowd of people.

The glob began to bubble and move again.
All at once, Tony, Orlando, and Dawn popped
out. They were fine, also.

"Yippee!" cheered the crowd of people.

Finally, the glob bubbled and moved one last time, and Mr. Meaner popped his head out. He was back to his old self, too.

"Awwww, MAAAN!" moaned the crowd of people.

CHAPTER 37
BACK TO NORMAL

George and Harold woke up to the rising
sun and looked out their tree house window.

"The whole city looks like it's back to
normal," said George.

"Even the stinky brown clouds have
disappeared!" said Harold.

It was a good thing, too, because George's and Harold's colds had finally gone away.

The two friends climbed down from their tree house and looked in Harold's bedroom window. Yesterday Harold was still sound asleep. Soon, the Rid-O-Kid 2000™ would wear off, and Yesterday George and Yesterday Harold would be back to normal.

George and Harold walked out to the front yard, where they saw some familiar faces.

"What happened?" cried Harold. "Is everything OK?"

"Of course it is," said Old George.

"Yeah," said Old Harold. "Adults can be heroes, too, you know!"

Old George and Old Harold told their younger selves all about their great adventure while they walked toward Echo Hills together.

On the way, they passed Mr. Krupp. He was outside in his yard raking the grass as a jogger ran by snapping her fingers.

SNAP! SNAP! SNAP! SNAP! SNAP! SNAP!

"You stay away from my yard!" Mr. Krupp shouted.

"What's going on?" cried Harold. "Mr. Krupp just heard somebody snap their fingers, and he DIDN'T turn into you-know-who!"

"I have no idea how that happened," said Old George.

Perhaps it was the electromagnetic pulse that erased the hypnotic spell from Mr. Krupp's brain. Or maybe it happened during the Super-Power-Juice-*ectomy*. Nobody knew for sure, but for some strange reason, Mr. Krupp was now back to normal, too.

Soon our heroes arrived at Echo Hills and prepared to return to the future.

"Thanks for all of your help last night," said George.

"Yeah," said Harold. "You guys did a pretty good job—for old people."

"PRETTY GOOD?!!?" cried Old Harold.

"*OLD* PEOPLE?!!?" cried Old George.

CHAPTER 38
HOME AGAIN,
NATURALLY

Suddenly, there was a blinding flash of light.
Twenty years flashed forward in an instant, and
the empty hilltop was now filled with homes
and trees. Old George's and Old Harold's
families were all there, too, anxiously waiting
for their return.

It was a joyful reunion.

"Well," said Harold, "I think we'd better go back home."

"You know," said George, "we don't actually *have* to go home."

"What do you mean?" asked Harold.

"We've got our own time machine," said George. "We could go anywhere we want! We can explore time together. We can go on awesome new adventures!"

"Wow!" said Harold. "That sounds like fun!"

"What should we do first?" asked Harold.

"Let's go rescue Crackers and Sulu,"
said George. The three baby hamsterdactyls
flapped their wings with excitement.

"How in the world are we ever going to
do that?" asked Harold.

"We'll figure something out," said George,
as he set the controllers. "We always do!"

George and Harold and their happy pets
waved good-bye to their future families, and
together they all disappeared into a ball of
brilliant light.

A few hours had passed, and the Rid-O-Kid 2000™ had finally worn off.

Yesterday George and Yesterday Harold were back to their old selves again, but nothing around them seemed normal at all.

"I wonder where George and Harold went," said Yesterday George.

"I have no idea," said Yesterday Harold.

"And where did Tony, Orlando, and Dawn go?" asked Yesterday George.

"Beats me," said Yesterday Harold. "It seems like they just disappeared."

Yesterday George and Yesterday Harold didn't know what had happened, or why everything had turned out OK. But it seemed like things were going to be just fine from now on, and they were very grateful.

"Well, what should we do now?" asked
Harold.

"Let's make a new comic book," said
George.

"About Captain Underpants?" asked
Harold.

"Nah," said George. "Let's do something
different. How about a Dog Man comic?"

"OK," said Harold happily.

And together, the two friends
wrote and drew and laughed
all afternoon.

★ *"Irreverent, laugh-out-loud funny, and . . . downright moving."*
— Publishers Weekly, starred review

ABOUT THE
AUTHOR-ILLUSTRATOR

When Dav Pilkey was a kid, he was diagnosed with ADHD and dyslexia. Dav was so disruptive in class that his teachers made him sit out in the hallway every day. Luckily, Dav loved to draw and make up stories. He spent his time in the hallway creating his own original comic books — the very first adventures of Dog Man and Captain Underpants.

In college, Dav met a teacher who encouraged him to write and illustrate for kids. He took her advice and created his first book, WORLD WAR WON, which won a national competition in 1986. Dav made many other books before being awarded the California Young Reader Medal for DOG BREATH (1994) and the Caldecott Honor for THE PAPERBOY (1996).

In 2002, Dav published his first full-length graphic novel for kids, called THE ADVENTURES OF SUPER DIAPER BABY. It was both a USA Today and New York Times bestseller. Since then, he has published more than a dozen full-length graphic novels for kids, including the bestselling Dog Man and Cat Kid Comic Club series.

Dav's stories are semi-autobiographical and explore universal themes that celebrate friendship, empathy, and the triumph of the good-hearted.

When he is not making books for kids, Dav loves to kayak with his wife in the Pacific Northwest.

Learn more at Pilkey.com.